W9-CEE-197

Woody Guthrie
NEW BABY TRAIN

Illustrated by Marla Frazee

Megan Tingley Books
LITTLE, BROWN AND COMPANY
New York ∾ Boston

To Olivia Nora Irion, who just came in on the new baby train
—Nora Guthrie

To Gwen, the Godmother and more...
—Marla Frazee

The publisher wishes to thank Nora Guthrie, Larry Richmond, and Judy Bell for their
creative assistance with this project. For more information about Woody Guthrie,
contact www.woodyguthrie.org.

Woody Guthrie® is a U.S. registered trademark of Woody Guthrie Publications. Used by permission.
Signature image courtesy of Woody Guthrie Archives.

"New Baby Train" copyright © 1999 by Ludlow Music, Inc., New York, N.Y.
International copyright secured. All rights reserved including public performance
for profit. Used by permission of Ludlow Music, Inc.

Illustrations copyright © 2004 by Marla Frazee
All rights reserved. No part of this book may be reproduced in any form or by any electronic or mechanical means, including information storage and retrieval systems, without permission in writing from the publisher,
except by a reviewer who may quote brief passages in a review.

Little, Brown and Company

Time Warner Book Group
1271 Avenue of the Americas, New York, NY 10020
Visit our Web site at www.lb-kids.com

First Edition

Library of Congress Cataloging-in-Publication Data
Guthrie, Woody, 1912–1967.
  New baby train / words by Woody Guthrie; illustrated by Marla Frazee.—1st ed.
    p. cm.
  Summary: An illustrated version of the song that answers the question "Where do little babies really
come from?"
  ISBN 0-316-07203-6
  1. Children's songs—United States—Texts. [1. Babies—Songs and music. 2. Songs.] I. Frazee, Marla, ill.
II. Title.

PZ8.3.G9635Ne 2004
782.42164'0268—de21   2003044726

10 9 8 7 6 5 4 3 2 1

Book design by Alyssa Morris

SC

Manufactured in China

The illustrations for this book were done in gouache on French recycled Speckletone.
The text was set in Opti Powell Old Style, and the display type was hand-lettered by Marla Frazee.

You know, a lot of people ask me,
I bet you'd like to know,
"How do brand-new babies
get into this house?"

You know I've got the same question.
Where do little babies really come from?

The flowers bring some,

the trees bring some,

the birds bring some,

the cars bring some,

and everything else brings some.
I guess maybe the trains bring some.

I guess little babies come along
just about any way they can.
Cars, trucks, tractors, airplanes,
any way they can come.

But here's the way they might come . . .
on a train.
Sort of a new baby train!

Here's the way it looks when it's standing still
waitin' for the conductor to tell it to start up.

All the little babies are lookin' out the windows
wonderin' which house they're
gonna get off at, you know?

"Hey Mister Conductor
I'm sitting here waitin'.
How long do I have to wait?
I sure do wanna go, I sure do wanna go,
I sure do wanna go on that new baby train."

The conductor says, "Okay,

you can go ahead now."

So the train starts up kinda slow
blowin' the whistle and lettin' out steam.

And it looks like this:

I wanna go faster

I wanna go faster

I wanna go faster!

Okay, this new baby train's got all the track to itself.
So you can go just as fast as you want to.

Over a big high mountain
way up through the clouds and back down again

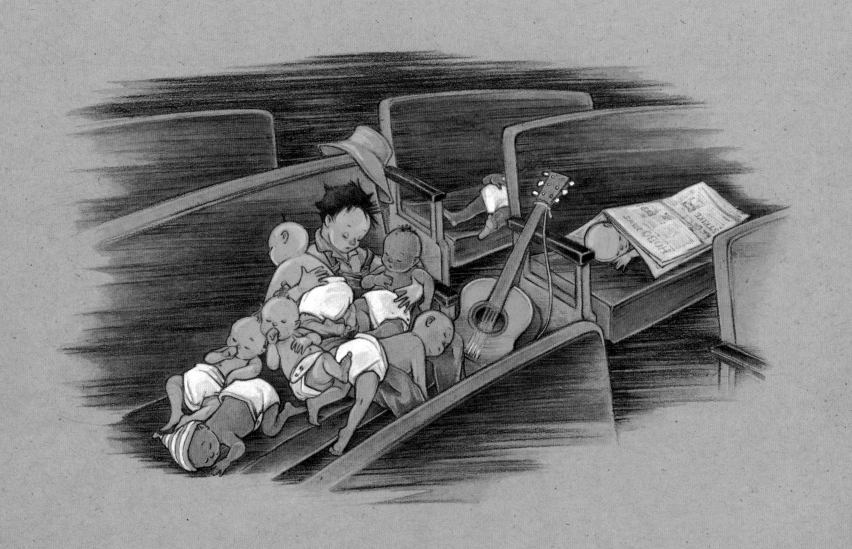

through the sky and everywhere else...

to let all the babies off at their homes.

You know, everyone is gonna be so happy.
All these babies are goin' home.

Oh, a lot of people ask me,
I bet you'd like to know.
"How do brand-new babies
Get into this house?"

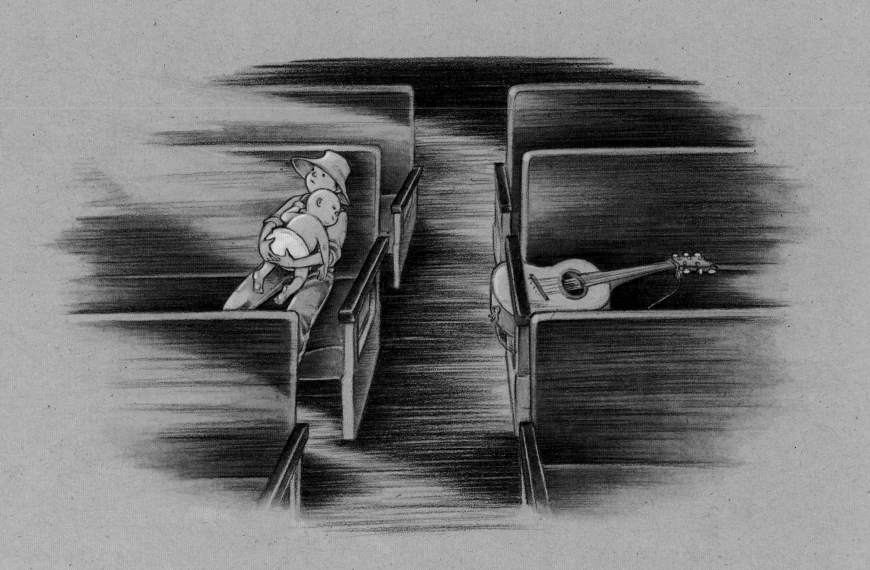

On the new baby train!